Young Amy

Young Animal Pride Series
Book 15

Cataloging-in-Publication Data

Sargent, Dave, 1941–
    Young amy / by Dave and Pat Sargent ;
illustrated by Elaine Woodword.—Prairie Grove, AR :
Ozark Publishing, c2005.
        p. cm.   (Young animal pride series ; 15)

        "Pay attention"—Cover.
        SUMMARY: Amy gets lost while
she's practicing eating grasshoppers. She
meets a bobcat, also lost. Billy Beaver
gets them back to their mamas.
        ISBN 1-56763-891-0 (hc)
                1-56763-892-9 (pbk)

        1. Armadillos—Juvenile fiction.
[1. Armadillos—Fiction.] I. Sargent, Pat, 1936–
II. Woodword, Elaine, 1956– ill. III. Title.
IV. Series.

        PZ10.3.S243Am 2005
        [Fic]—dc21   2004093001

Printed in the United States of America

Young Amy

Young Animal Pride Series
Book 15

by Dave and Pat Sargent

Illustrated by Elaine Woodword

Ozark Publishing, Inc.
P.O. Box 228
Prairie Grove, AR 72753

Dave and Pat Sargent, authors of the extremely popular Animal Pride Series, visit schools all over the United States, free of charge. If you would like to have Dave and Pat visit your school, please ask your librarian to call 1-800-321-5671.

Foreword

While Amy Armadillo is practicing how to catch grasshoppers, she gets lost. Amy meets a bobcat who's lost, too. After scary adventures, a beaver friend helps them find their mamas.

My name is Amy.

I am an armadillo.

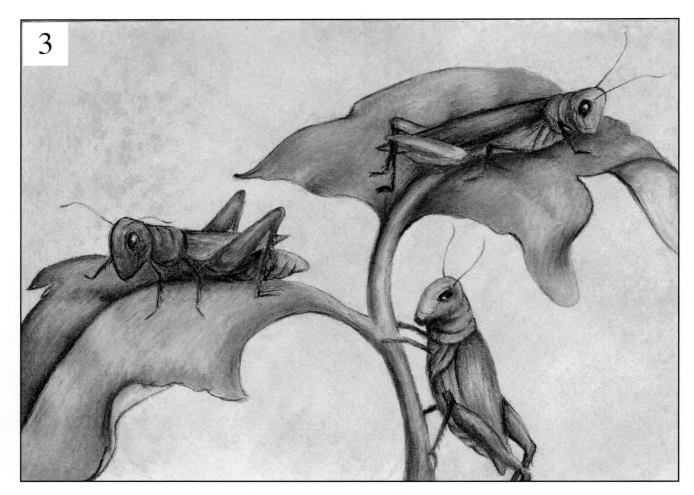

I catch grasshoppers.

I use my tongue!

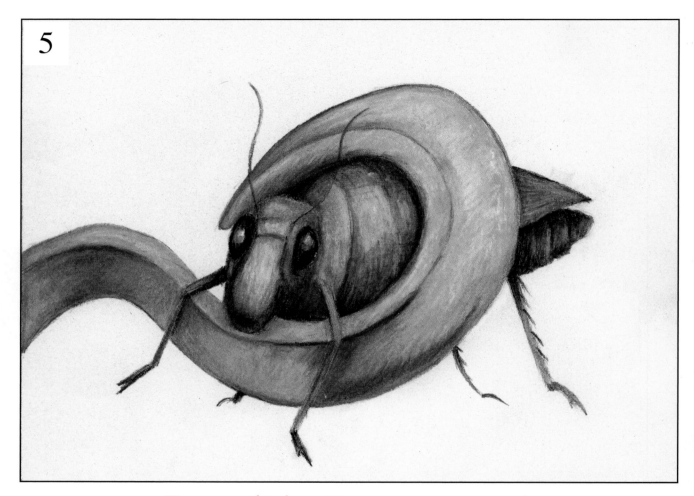

Look! I got one!

It is good!

I am lost!

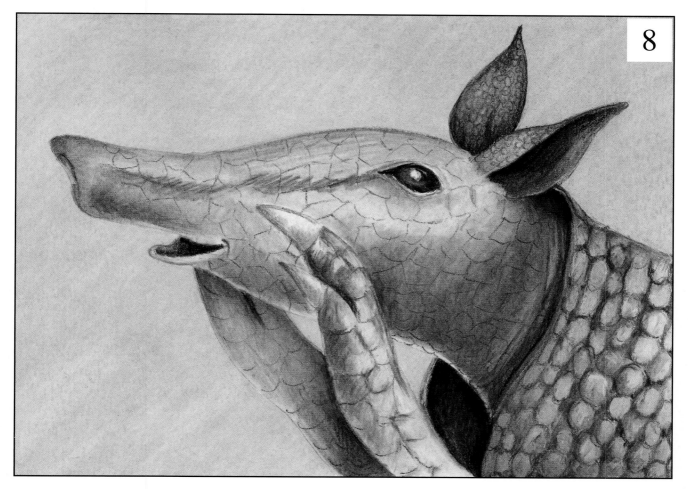

Mama! Where are you?

I see Bob.

Bob is lost, too.

We can play.

We play on a log.

The log floats away.

We are scared.

We go down the rapids.

We hit Billy's lodge.

We are lost, Billy.

Billy Beaver helps us.

Billy finds our mamas.